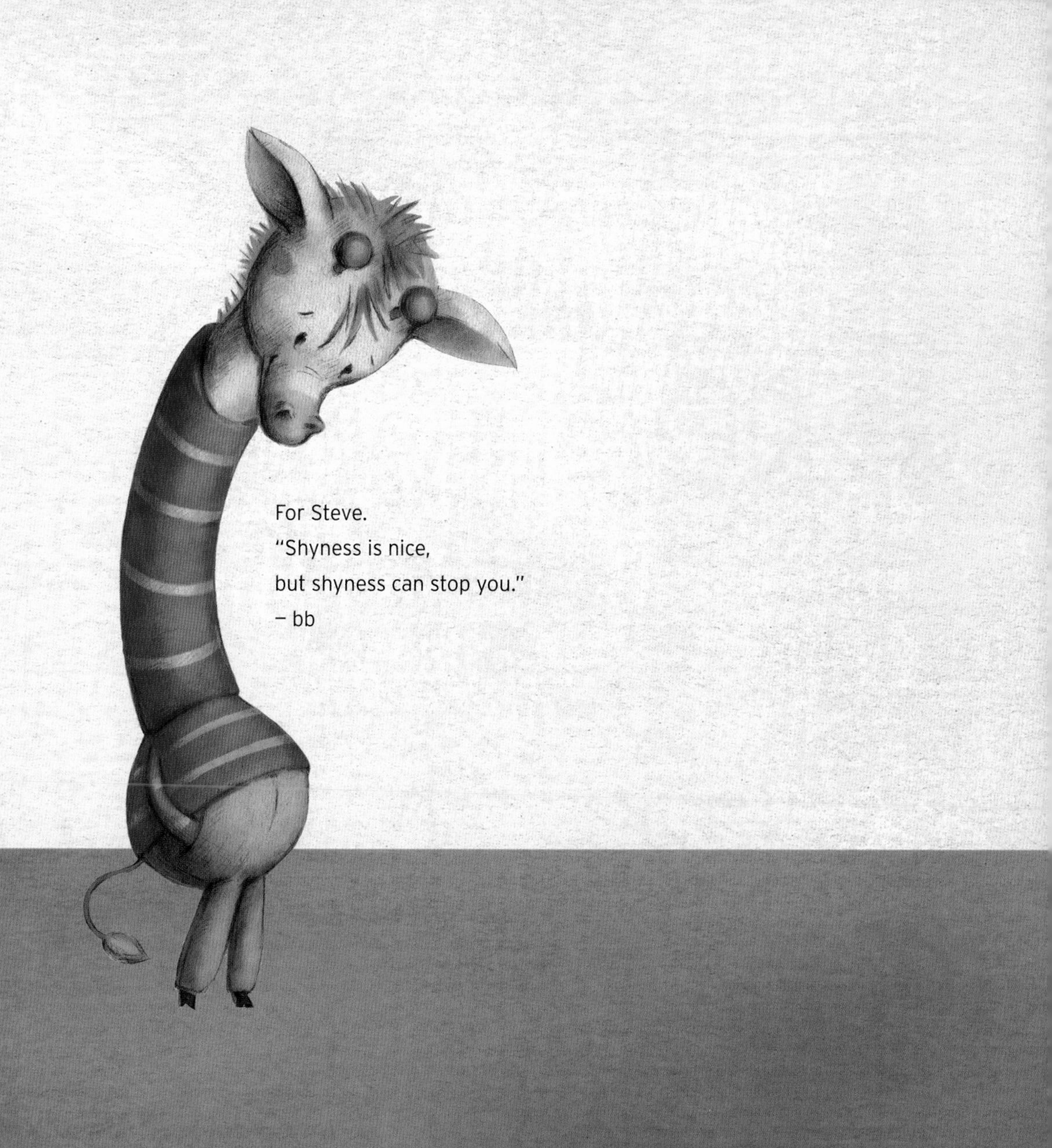

For Steve.

"Shyness is nice,
but shyness can stop you."
– bb

Little Boost is published by
Picture Window Books
A Capstone Imprint
1710 Roe Crest Drive
North Mankato, Minnesota 56003
www.capstonepub.com

Library of Congress Cataloging-in-Publication data is available on the Library of Congress website.

ISBN 978-1-4048-7418-3

Art Director: Kay Fraser
Designer: Emily Harris

Printed in China. 102011 006443

Too Shy for Show-and-Tell

by Beth Bracken

illustrated by Jennifer Bell

PICTURE WINDOW BOOKS
a capstone imprint

Sam was a quiet boy.
Nobody knew much about him.

Sam loved trucks, but nobody knew that.

Sam's favorite food was chocolate cake,
but nobody knew that.

Sam thought dogs were the best animals in the world, but nobody knew that, either.

The only thing that people knew about Sam was that he didn't talk much.

And Sam really didn't like talking in front of people,
which is why Sam hated show-and-tell.

On Wednesday, Miss Emily told the class that show-and-tell would be on Friday.

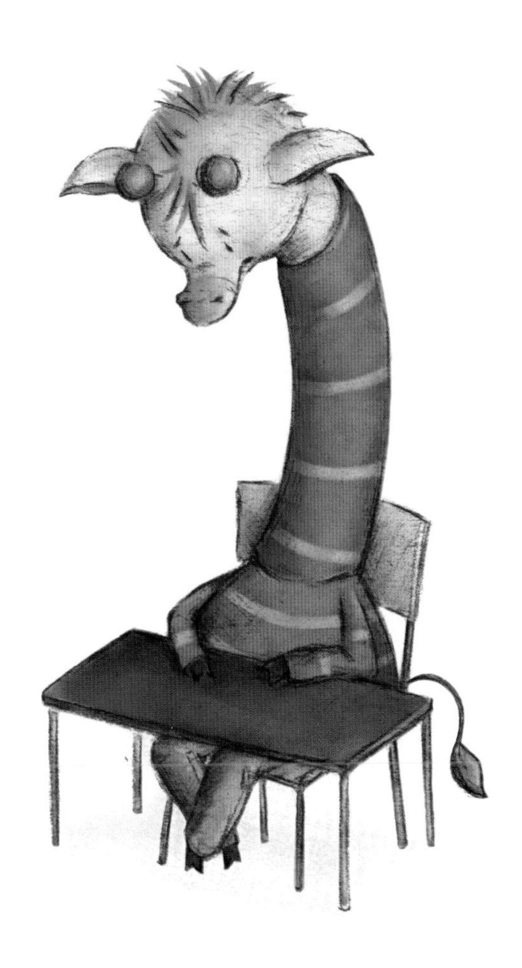

Sam spent most of Thursday worrying. He had a great thing to bring for show-and-tell, but he was scared.

On Friday, Sam didn't get out of bed.
"My tummy hurts," he lied.

"You're fine, and you need to go to school today," his mom said.

At school, Sam told Miss Emily he'd forgotten about show-and-tell.

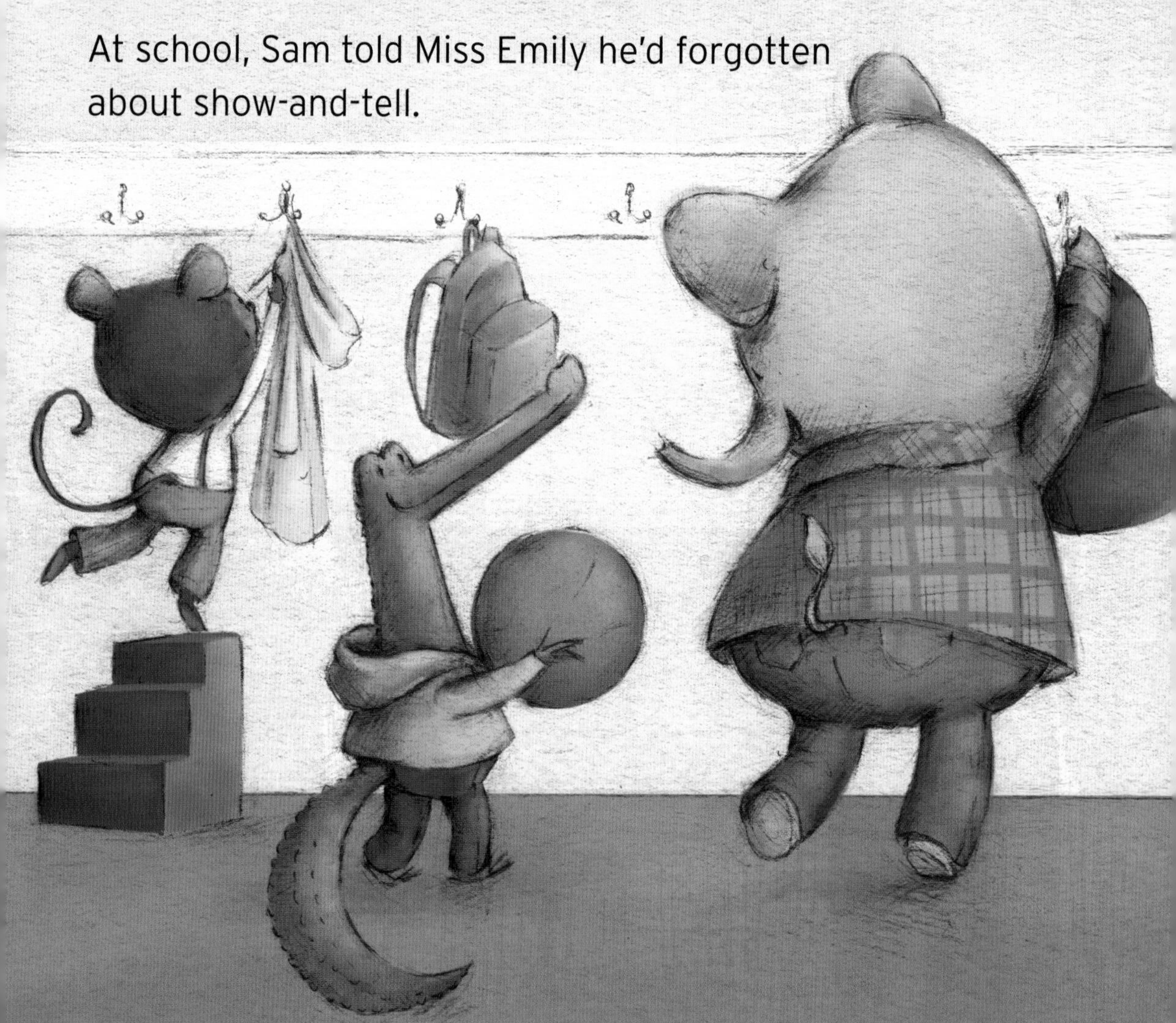

"I didn't bring anything," he said. But that wasn't true. His perfect show-and-tell thing was in his backpack.

"That's okay," Miss Emily said. "You can just tell the class about the thing you forgot at home."

Sam was terrified. He didn't want to talk in front of everyone.
The thought of it made his tummy hurt really, really bad.

He imagined that he'd say something dumb.

Or that he'd mess up his words.

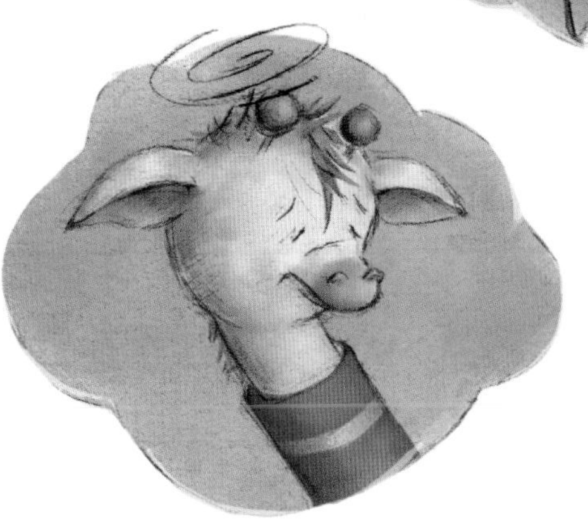

Or that he'd faint.

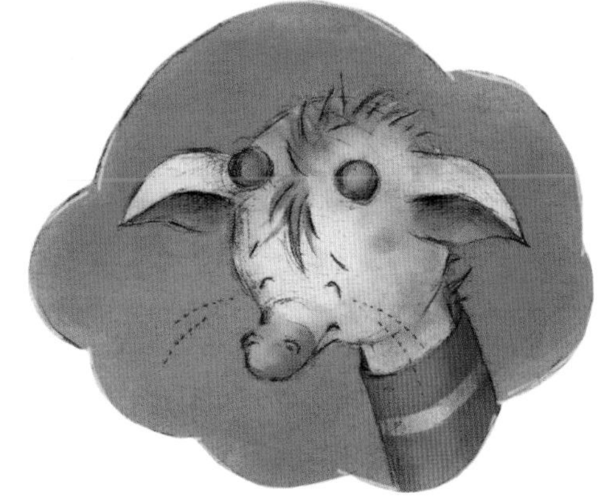

Or that he'd cry.

Sam watched the other kids show their
show-and-tell things.

David showed some socks that his grandma had knitted him.
Everyone clapped when he was done.

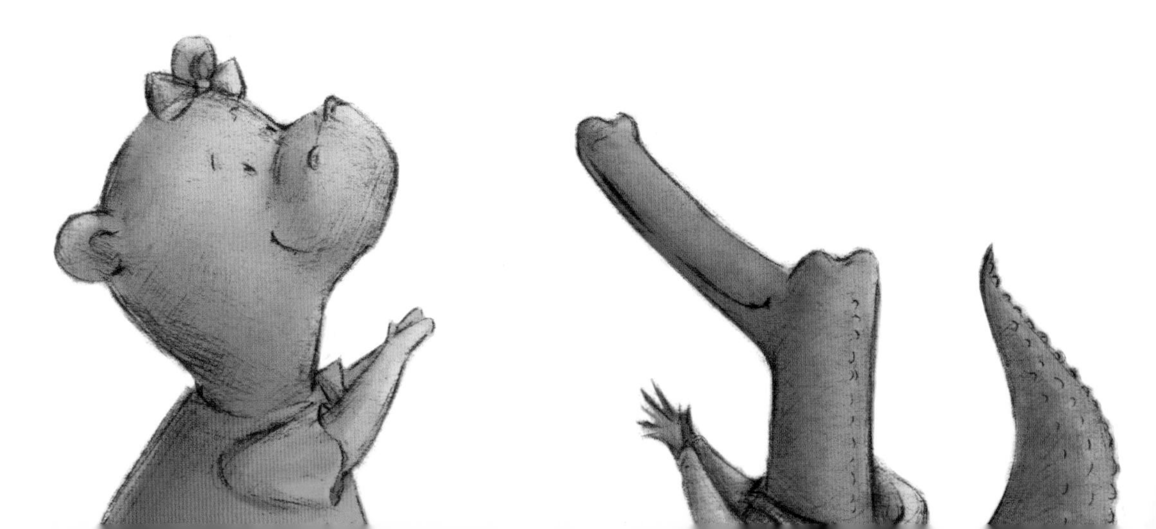

Helena showed a new doll she got for her birthday.
Everyone clapped when she was done.

Otto showed a cool leaf that he found on the way to school. He said "weaf" instead of "leaf," but nobody cared.

And everyone clapped when he was done.

Then it was Sam's turn. He got his perfect show-and-tell thing out of his backpack and went to the front of the room.

"What do you have to show us today, Sam?"
Miss Emily asked with a smile.

Sam took a deep breath. He looked out at his classmates. They were quietly waiting.

Sam held up his picture. "This is my new dog," he said. "I named him Chocolate, because that's my favorite kind of cake, and he's the color of chocolate cake."

Sam didn't faint.

He didn't throw up.

He didn't cry.

And no one laughed.

Instead, everyone clapped
when he was done.

Now everyone in class knew
a little bit more about Sam.

Next time, he thought,
I'll bring my biggest truck.